Paradise Press, Inc

Exclusive distribution by Paradise Press, Inc.
© Creation, text and illustrations: A.M. Lefèvre, M. Loiseaux,
M. Nathan-Deiller, A. Van Gool
This 1999 edition produced by ADC International, Belgium
and published by Ottenheimer Publishers, Inc.,
Owings Mills, Maryland. All rights reserved.
SCO63MLKJIHGFEDCBA

Printed in Indonesia

The Ugly Duckling

'''VAN GOOL'''

Mother Duck sat patiently on her eggs. She was keeping them warm until they hatched. "When are those ducklings coming out?" asked Mother Duck's friend. Mother Duck smiled. "It takes a long time," she replied. "They'll hatch when they're ready."

Just then, Mother Duck heard a *pick peck pick*, then a *crackety crack*. Soon her ducklings pecked and scratched their way out of the eggs. They looked about and blinked their big eyes at the bright light.

Mother Duck peered at them happily. "Hello, little darlings," she said.

The little yellow ducklings quacked excitedly to each other in their tiny voices. The last duckling was still struggling out of his shell. Finally he emerged, craned his long neck and gave a loud *honk*. Mother Duck looked at him closely.

The last duckling was different from the others. He was gray instead of yellow, and his large size made him a bit clumsy. He honked instead of chirping.

"Goodness!" exclaimed Mother Duck. The smaller ducklings glanced at each other with surprise. A bit of shell still clung to the large duckling's head, making him look comical. The little ducklings began to giggle.

Soon the other barnyard birds joined
the laughter. They snickered and
pointed unkindly at the ugly duckling.

"Stop your foolish laughter!" quacked Mother Duck angrily. She hustled her babies out of the barn and down the slope to a little pond. There the ducklings had their first swim, splashing merrily as they floated about like little corks.

Mother Duck climbed out of the pond. As soon as their mother had left, the little ducklings turned to the big one. "You're not one of us!" hissed one of them.

"You're the ugly duckling," chirped another.

The other barnyard fowl came to make fun of the unhappy duckling.

The ugly duckling huddled under his mother's wing.
"You should be ashamed of yourselves," quacked Mother Duck angrily, "picking on a helpless little duckling. Leave him alone!"

But the commotion only got worse, as the turkey and other ducks and chickens joined the squabble. "He's got to go!" they honked and clucked and quacked. Not even the ugly duckling's mother could protect him.

The ugly duckling found an opening in the wall and fled across the meadow. The loud birds followed him a short distance. Then he could hear their angry voices as he darted under the fence and stumbled into the forest.

21

The ugly duckling was afraid. Was it his fault that he didn't look like the others? Before long he noticed that the forest was growing darker and colder. "I'll just have to take care of myself," he said. He made a grassy nest under a big tree, and passed his first long night alone, trying not to think of his mother's soft feathers and kind eyes.

The ugly duckling awoke shivering with the cold. He felt lonely and hungry and not at all brave. He began to cry.

"Hi, there," said a field mouse, who had come to see who was sobbing. "I'm Tim and this here's Tom. What are you doing out here by yourself?"
The duckling told his sad story to the kind mice.

25

"Maybe you could be friends with that fellow over there," suggested Tom, pointing to a heron in a nearby pond.

"I'll give it a try," responded the ugly duckling doubtfully. He waddled to the water's edge.

The heron was not at all
friendly. When he stood up,
his legs were so long that he
loomed over the duckling,
who turned and fled.

"What you need," said Tim, "is to be with your own kind." He and Tom urged the duckling towards the ducks in a nearby pond.

But when the duckling approached the strange ducks, he was not greeted warmly. The ducklings jeered at him, and the big duck splashed him, quacking, "Go away!"

The duckling was about to cry, when a dog burst through the underbrush.

"It's the hunter's dog!" cried Tom. "Let's get out of here!"

"Wait for me!" quacked the duckling. He ran as fast as his little legs could carry him, following his friends to safety.

"Whew! That was a close one," said Tim, when they were sure the dog was not chasing them.

"Look," exclaimed Tom, "a farmhouse! Our little friend would be safe here."

The duckling looked at the cheerful farmhouse in the clearing.

The mice urged the duckling to the farmhouse door. When the farmer's wife came out to milk the cow, she scooped up the little duckling. "Are you lost?" she asked gently. While the mice watched, she carried him into the house.

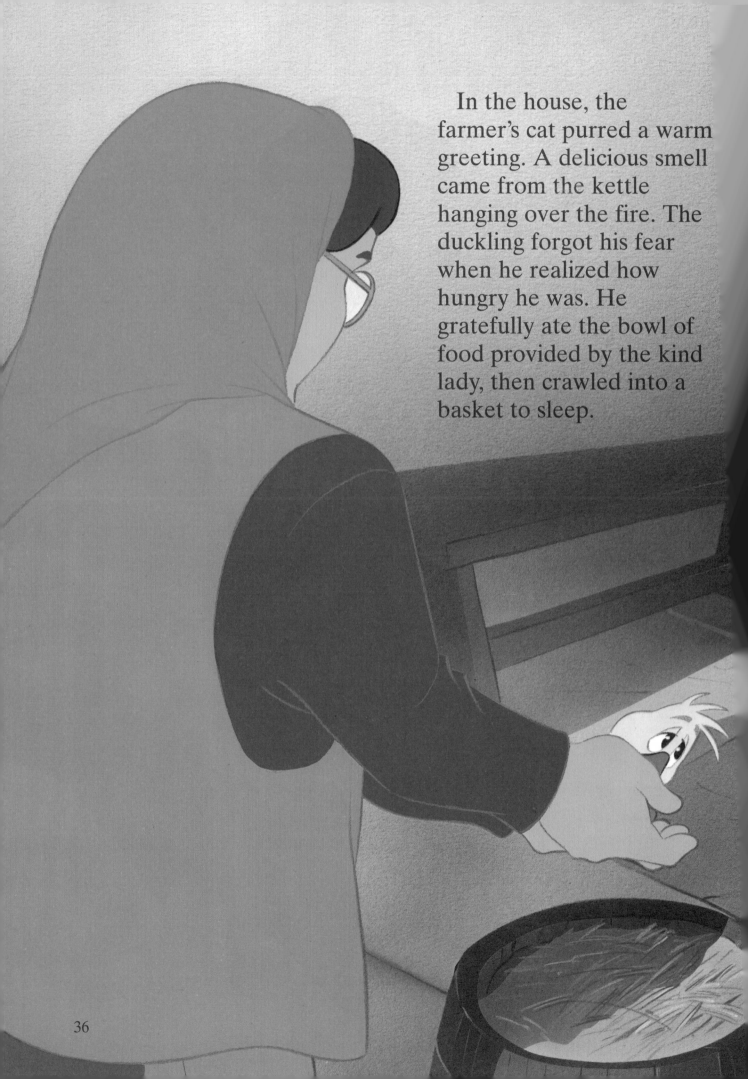

In the house, the farmer's cat purred a warm greeting. A delicious smell came from the kettle hanging over the fire. The duckling forgot his fear when he realized how hungry he was. He gratefully ate the bowl of food provided by the kind lady, then crawled into a basket to sleep.

The duckling enjoyed the kindness of the lady and her cat. But as the days and weeks passed, he began to feel uneasy in the small house.
He longed to swim on the water and feel the breeze ruffle his feathers.
He missed his friends the mice, who sometimes came to peer at him through the window.

One day, when the farmer's wife opened
the door, the duckling rushed out. The
three friends ran across the meadow.

The duckling and mice passed the summer on the lakeshore, playing tag and blindman's buff. Soon autumn arrived, and the cool, windy weather made the duckling feel uneasy. One day he saw some beautiful white birds flying south, and he longed to join them. But he couldn't yet fly, so he and the mice went looking for a warm place to spend the winter.

Winter came as suddenly as the snow one night, and in the morning laughter rang through the air as the duckling and the mice slid down a hill, and shook snow off the trees on to each other. The woods and meadow looked beautiful cloaked in white, but winter was not so much fun later that day, when it turned bitterly cold.

The cold weather brought a blizzard, which caught the duckling by surprise. Separated from his friends, he became lost as he trudged through the snow.

Finally the duckling spotted a barn, but he was so cold and exhausted that he collapsed in the snow. He would have frozen if his friends hadn't found him.

"We've got to get help fast," said Tom. "Quick, run and get the barn mice."

Tim scrambled to the barn, and before long he returned with the barn mice.

The mice heaved and pulled and pushed the duckling through the snow, until at last they managed to get him into the barn.

Tim and Tom were afraid that their friend might never awaken. Lovingly, they made him a nest of straw, and huddled close to him through the long night.

When morning came the mice cheered to see the
duckling awake. While he listened quietly, the excited
mice told how they had rescued him from the blizzard.

"You're the best friends a duck could have," the duckling said to Tim and Tom. "And thanks," he added to the barn mice.
The friends decided to spend the rest of the winter in the barn. They passed the days playing games and singing.

When spring came the duckling, Tim and Tom decided to return to their homes by the lake. They thanked the barn mice for their help and friendship, and set off across the meadow, waving goodbye.

When the friends slipped under the fence at the edge of the farm, the ugly duckling suddenly began to cry.

"What is it?" asked Tom. The duckling had remembered the big, graceful birds he had seen flying south in the fall. All winter their beauty had haunted him. When he told the mice, they tried to cheer him up. "Those were swans you saw," said Tim. "They should be back any day now. I'm sure they'll want you to join them."

Just then they heard a honking overhead, and looked up to see the swans circling over the lake. The beautiful creatures landed on the water.

"Come over here!" cried Tim to the duckling. "I've got something to show you!"

The duckling joined
the mice at the water's
edge. He caught his
breath. The swans were
watching him. The shy
duckling felt sure the
swans would not
welcome him.

"My goodness, look at your reflection!" exclaimed Tim. The duckling craned his neck to look into the still water. The water's glassy surface was a perfect mirror, and in it the reflection he saw was not that of any ugly duckling at all, but that of a beautiful swan!

Suddenly, he realized why he had never fitted in with the ducks: he had been born a swan. He hardly noticed that the mice had climbed aboard his back. Quickly, he paddled out to greet the swans, his heart pounding.

The other swans stared with surprise when he approached, and the ugly duckling expected the worst. But instead, they stroked his feathers with their bills, accepting him as one of their own. No one was happier at that moment than the devoted mice and the once ugly duckling, who had turned into the most beautiful swan of all.